THE SEARCH

Eric Heuvel | Ruud van der Rol | Lies Schippers

THE SEARCH

ANNE FRANK HOUSE

in cooperation with the Jewish Historical Museum of Amsterdam

Farrar Straus Giroux / New York

Esther's parents,
Dr. and Mrs. Hecht

Esther

Helena van Dort

Bob's parents,
Mr. and Mrs. Canter

Bob

Esther and her grandson, Daniel

Helena and her grandson, Jeroen

Bob

Esther's son, Paul, lives in
the Netherlands. Esther is visiting from
the United States to celebrate her grandson Daniel's
Bar Mitzvah. She also wants to spend time with her
long-lost friend Helena and introduce Daniel to
Helena's grandson, Jeroen.

Jeroen is off to his gran's house.

I'm glad they asked me to go!

Ah, Jeroen, you're right on time. Esther's also here.

Hello!

My grandson, Daniel, is excited you're coming with us.

So, we're visiting the farm where you were in hiding during the war?

Yes, there was a terrible incident... I'm ready to find out what finally happened.

That must be my son, Paul, here to pick us up.

I'll get it...

Ringgg

You're Jeroen?

Yes!

Daniel, is that you? I hardly recognize you without your tie!

How's that?

Oh, I made my Bar Mitzvah last week.

Huh?

7

In the Jewish religion a Bar Mitzvah means you become an adult. At our synagogue, for the first time, I read aloud from the Torah.

ושננתם לבניך ודברת בם בשבתך בביתך ובלכתך * בדרך ובשכבך ובקומך.

*You shall teach these words diligently to your children and speak of them always...

Phew... that went well!

It's also a celebration.

A new skateboard!

Mazzeltov Daniël!

You must be Daniel's grandmother...

I came all the way from the U.S. just for this occasion...

Back in the living room...

I couldn't have missed Daniel's Bar Mitzvah.

C'mon, Mom, we should get going...

A while later...

The people who hid me at that time had a son. He's still alive. His name is Barend. I thought he was so brave...

But such terrible things happened back then...

Are you certain you want to do this, Mom?

Wenn schon, denn schon...

Excuse me?

That was my father's favorite saying. It's German for "If you do something, then do it well."

Your grandma lived in Germany until she was twelve.

My father was a family doctor in Karlsruhe. My mother was a teacher until I was born in 1926.

My mother absolutely loved taking pictures...

My grandparents lived in a nearby city.

But life was very hard in Germany back then.

Unemployment and poverty kept increasing.

I have patients who are ill from all their distress.

Mom, why are all those people standing in line?

They don't have jobs. The government gives them money.

WÄHLT HITLER

Many people were desperate.

Please, give me a loaf of bread. My wife and children are hungry. I'll pay you next week.

No, pay now. I need to make a living too.

Elections were held. Hitler became the leader of the Nazi Party.

U-N-S-E-R-E L-E-T-Z-T-E H-O-F-F-N-U-N-G... H-I-T-L-E-R*
What does that mean, Mom?

He's got my vote!

At least he has a vision...

*Our Last Hope: Hitler

What's wrong, Mom?

What nonsense! Bunch of fools!

9

I remember my mother getting so angry because more and more people supported Adolf Hitler and his Nazi Party.

But what made them support Hitler?

All his promises...

I will see to it that there is work again! There will be an end to poverty!

Fantastic!

Finally!

Heil Hitler!

He wanted a powerful German empire.

Germany must become a great and strong nation again, so every German can be proud!

We Germans are the best race on earth. Our race must become purer and stronger...

Well said!

Exactly!

Why is the situation in Germany so bad? It's the fault of the Jews! Not only are they a danger to the purity of our race, they want to destroy Germany! They are the greatest enemy of the German people!

Hitler blamed the Jews for all the country's misery. He made us into scapegoats.

What the Nazis are saying about Jews is utterly absurd!

Oh, most people don't believe all that Nazi nonsense...

But my father was wrong. Hitler's Nazi party continued to gain strength.

But Hitler also had opponents. There were frequent street fights.

Let's go, Esther!

In 1933, Hitler became head of the government.

Everything will be better now!

There were celebrations all across Germany.

Listeners... the crowd cannot contain its enthusiasm. Adolf Hitler will lead Germany...

...to a beautiful future!

What will happen now?

Hitler got rid of democracy. He became a dictator. His opponents were beaten up or imprisoned in concentration camps.

It's not like Hitler didn't warn them? If you're not with him, you're against him.

People were no longer allowed to frequent Jewish shops.

Don't you even think about buying something here!

Deutsche! Wehrt Euch! kauft nicht bei Juden

Jewish civil servants were dismissed—even my grandpa who worked at the post office.

They just fired me...

After all these years?!!

Now they are saying I can only treat Jewish patients.

But almost all your patients are non-Jews! How are we going to manage?

Were all Germans against the Jews?

No, not everyone was anti-Semitic.

I feel terrible about not being your patient anymore... I'm...

You're scared...

I had a non-Jewish friend who lived next door, Fritz.

Let's do our home-work together?

Okay.

Fritz's father was the local baker.

Look, Esther...

Cookies! Yummy!

Fritz and I usually walked to school together.

We're getting a new teacher today.

I heard she's a Nazi.

But our friendship soon came to an end.

Are you okay, Mom?

C'mon, let's stop for a quick coffee.

A while later...

Gran, what happened next?

€ 4,=

The new teacher made me sit apart from my classmates.

Remember, children: Jews are our enemy. These are the very words of our leader, Adolf Hitler.

Der Jude ist unser größte Feind
$ = ✡ = ☭

After school...

Join us, Fritzy boy?

No, I promised I'd help my father...

Jew... Jew!

Bullies!

Once safely at home...

I'm going to that school...

No, don't. You'll only make things worse...

Sob, sob...

One day, Fritz's father turned up in his Nazi uniform.

It suits you well...

Sharp, huh?

Fritz had to join the Hitlerjugend, the Nazi Youth League.

I don't want you hanging around with that Jew girl anymore... Understood?!

Yes, Father.

Fritz isn't allowed to see you anymore!

Things kept getting worse.

Just keep walking.

Ich bin ein Rasseschänder

Race polluter? Because he's in love with a Jewish woman?

In 1935, race laws were declared.

Marriages and relationships with Jews are now forbidden.

Juden sind hier unerwünscht!*

C'mon, we're almost home.

*Jews Not Wanted Here!

Why did you stick it out so long?

Germany was our country. We felt German.

After November 9, 1938, we wanted to leave. That night, the Nazis organized a violent campaign against Germany's Jews.

There's a Jewish shop!

Oh no, that's Fritz's father!

On Kristallnacht, the "Night of Broken Glass," more than 100 Jews were murdered and many Jewish shops destroyed.

seit 1894

Is that necessary?

It's their own fault!

That'll teach you, dirty Jew!

Hundreds of synagogues were destroyed or set on fire.

This has gone too far. It's still a house of God...

The next day, more than 30,000 Jews were rounded up. Our neighbor was among them.

These people are all decent citizens!

Shut up! After all, they're Jews!

They were imprisoned in concentration camps. There they were humiliated and mistreated.

Deeper, bend those knees deeper...

What will they do with us?

A week later, we heard from our neighbor's wife that her husband had died in the camp.

Sob... sob...

He was perfectly healthy...

My parents wanted to leave Germany as quickly as possible. But that was difficult.

Where can we go? Not one country is prepared to accept more Jewish refugees!

Perhaps my Amsterdam colleague Professor Bouwer can help us.

We were fortunate. The Netherlands had also closed its borders to refugees, but sometimes exceptions were made.

It's arranged! We're going to Holland!

We were only allowed to take a few suitcases.

Hurry, dear! That train won't wait!

This was my grand-mother's wardrobe!

Then you moved into the apartment in Gran's building?

Yes. Helena became my best friend.

Look, Esther, my diary... Go ahead, read it, really!

The Canter family lived a few doors down from us. They were also Jewish and had a son, Bob, who was older than me.

Delicious... What is it?

A Dutch specialty. Want the recipe?

I had a crush on Bob.

Ooooh, he's coming this way...

No, he's going to train at the boxing school. Let's go watch him.

There he is! Hey, Bob!

Don't do—

Huh?

POW!

Oops, sorry.

So much for that romance!

I quickly felt at home in the Netherlands.

Aren't you homesick?

At times. I mostly miss my grandparents.

My father was given work in a hospital. We felt safe in the Netherlands. But Hitler was intent on war...

15

In September 1939, the German Army, then the Russian Army, invaded Poland. World War II started.

My army and air force are invincible. The Poles will have no choice but to surrender!

In May 1940, Germany attacked the Netherlands too, even though it was neutral.

The Dutch military defense is a joke!

Going in for the kill!

We tried fleeing to England by boat.

Hurry up, the taxi's coming.

Sir, all the roads to the harbor are blocked.

Sigh... Then take us back to Amsterdam.

After the German bombardment of Rotterdam, the Dutch Army surrendered.

Now the Nazis also control the Netherlands.

Within a year, the Germans had figured out who was Jewish and exactly where the Jews lived.

Superb! Very clear overview!

We witnessed Dutch Nazis mistreating the Jews.

Animals!

But resistance grew. Jewish youngsters also fought back, and Bob took part.

You're selling rotten apples!

No, don't!

Let's help!

There were more and more street fights.

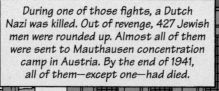

During one of those fights, a Dutch Nazi was killed. Out of revenge, 427 Jewish men were rounded up. Almost all of them were sent to Mauthausen concentration camp in Austria. By the end of 1941, all of them—except one—had died.

Many Amsterdamers were outraged. A strike broke out. But that "February Strike" was put down with violence.

It's hopeless.

Run! They're shooting!

There were signs saying "No Jews Allowed."

Another sign.

Ah, I wasn't in the mood to go to a movie anyway...

VERWACHT

Verboden voor Joden

Bob's boxing school membership was revoked.

BOKS SCHOOL

Sorry, Bob, but it's beyond my control.

VOOR JODEN VERBODEN

Grrrr...

Jews had to attend separate schools.

Let's try to make the best of it.

I miss Helena...

Jews from smaller towns were forced to move to Amsterdam.

JUDEN VIERTEL
JOODSCHE WIJK

Jewish Quarter. What are they up to?

Starting in May 1942, all Jews older than six had to wear a yellow star on their clothing.

I don't want this!

In July, more than 1,000 Jewish young people received a call-up for a labor camp in Germany.

Now we really have to do something.

We'll try to go into hiding.

17

But who can we trust?

Perhaps Professor Bouwer can help us again...

Times grew more and more dangerous. The Nazis would close off a street or neighborhood and arrest all the Jews.

Clear out! A razzia!

OPEN UP!

When they came, you could take only what you could carry.

I hope we'll hear from Professor Bouwer soon!

At school, teachers and students were disappearing.

Did you hear about Peter? He came home and his entire family had been taken away!

I think Hanna has gone into hiding.

A while longer, then hopefully I'll be in hiding too.

The day finally arrived...

Thank goodness! Bouwer has managed to arrange a hiding place.

When?

Next week, Tuesday.

I told Helena the news.

We're leaving soon.

I'm going to miss you.

Here, this necklace is for you. As a special token of our friendship.

My grandmother still wears that necklace! All the time!

But it all went wrong.

I left for school that day as usual.

Good luck with your test!

Thanks!

I should have studied harder...

I didn't realize at that moment that I was saying goodbye forever.

See you later, Esther!

Okay. Bye, Mom!

Later...

That went better than expected. Perhaps I even passed.

JOODSCH LYCEUM

Huh... what?

It was Helena's father. He worked for the police...

Hello, what's wrong?

Listen. Your parents have been picked up. Do you want to go to them or perhaps somewhere else?

It was a terribly difficult decision, but I finally decided to go to Professor Bouwer's house.

Esther, what is it? Quickly, inside!

RESTAUR

My parents were picked up while I was at school. So, now what?

Stay here tonight. I'll arrange for someone to take you to a hiding place tomorrow.

Hey... that policeman, was he your grandpa?

My great-grandfather. The father of my grandmother.

BLO

How do you feel about him now?

It's true he helped me, but he's also partly to blame for the death of my parents.

Oh...

The next day, someone from the Resistance came for me.

Good that you've come.

We need to change your appearance. Also, rip that yellow star off your coat.

Oooh...

Even with my new I.D. card, I was terrified in the train.

Oh no! Germans checking!

Pssst... remember, your new name is Hetty.

Relax. It's just some regular soldiers...

Phew...

We arrived at a village around dusk.

I was expecting three people. She has the money with her?

No, her parents were arrested.

Well, just one night then.

A few more hiding places followed...

Two people are already hiding here. Two nights, no more.

A pity...

I finally arrived at the farm we're going to visit today. I was able to stay there for more than six months.

I hope Barend will tell me how things turned out there.

Intertrans
BERLIN WARSZAWA

A half hour later...

Esther! Good to see you again. I've thought of you often over the years...

Barend!

You haven't changed a bit!

Haven't changed a bit!

Later...

I still remember the first time I saw you.

Yes, me too. I also remember the others who were hiding here.

A mother with two children. And a young teacher...

Nice to meet you. I'm Jacques.

Uh... I'm Hetty.

My wife and daughter are also in hiding... But I don't know where.

It's hard to believe I was actually in hiding here for more than six months!

What did you do the whole day, Gran? I'd be totally bored!

21

At times, we had to stay in the hayloft. If it was safe, we helped on the farm...

Glad to go outside, Barend!

All clear!

I liked helping and keeping busy. At least then I wasn't worried.

I can teach you to milk a cow?!

Please do!

It was harder than it looked...

No, you grab—

Oops, sorry!

Barend was a very nice young man. And I believe he liked me as well.

Sigh...

Oomph...

Ah, we were young...

If only I could have stayed...

Then one day... I will never forget it...

BrrrOOmmmm... rrrrrt...

What's that noise?

Oh no... NO!!!

22

23

I was so scared...

But... Tell me what happened exactly?

The Germans arrested all the people hiding here and also my father.

It's a miracle that they didn't arrest me too.

What happened to your father?

I never saw him again... He died in the Vught concentration camp.

How awful... Such a good man...

And the mother and her children? What happened to them?

I never heard anything from them again. They were probably murdered.

Why did you help people?

My family was very religious. We felt we were fulfilling our duty to God.

But now tell me what happened to you?

Sigh...

I didn't really know what to do. I was hungry... It was cold.

So... Where to now?

A house!

Hello, sir. I need a place to sleep...

I don't want any trouble...

Get out of here...!

Puff... Puff... What a bastard...

I kept going.

Hello. Could I work here in exchange for a bed and food?

Look at you! You'd better come in first.

You can spend the night here.

Thank you!

What's a girl like that doing out here, all alone?

That evening...

They're talking about me!

No doubt Jewish... on the run... help... dangerous... our duty... afraid...

The following morning...

You just stay awhile. There's plenty to do.

Thank you! I know how to milk a cow!

In October 1944, the South of the Netherlands was liberated...

The Americans are coming!

At last! Let's go see.

Long live the Queen!

No, she's not our niece, but a Jewish girl.

I need to go to Amsterdam to find my parents.

Of course. I hope they're okay.

But I had to wait 8 months. The North of the Netherlands was still occupied.

And? Did you find your parents?

Sigh... No, my parents were dead... murdered, that's the correct word!

But... how did you finally find out?

As soon as I could, I went to our apartment in Amsterdam.

The Hecht family? No, never heard of them...

What? And what about the Van Dorts?

They moved in with her aunt?

But nobody lived at Helena's aunt's address anymore...

No idea what happened to them...

Really?

I just moved here recently.

26

So then I went to Professor Bouwer.

Certainly you can stay. As long as you want.

Every day I went to the Central Train Station. Survivors from the camps returned there.

I'm trying to find my mother and father. He's a doctor. His name is Karl Hecht.

Don't know them...

More came to light about what had happened in the camps.

How dreadful!

I decided to take out an ad in the newspaper.

Your newspaper ad will appear as follows:

KARL HECHT born Feb. 5, 1899. MIRIAM HECHT-SILBER born March 12, 1901. Transported Oct. '43. Probably Auschwitz. Esther Hecht, Steenstraat 15, Amsterdam.

ADVERTENTIE AFDELING

Then one day...

Esther... Esther Hecht!

Uh... who are you...?

You... you're... Bob! Right? Bob Canter!!!

I survived the camps... I saw your ad in the paper...

Oh, Bob...! It's... It's so good to see you!

I don't know how to tell you this... Your parents are not coming back, Esther.

27

I heard Bob speaking, but I blocked out what he was saying.

....
....
....

Looking back now, there was so much more I wanted to ask. But I never saw him again. Maybe he went to live in Israel. That was his dream.

Bye, Esther.

I had to tell her...

So then you were all alone?

Sigh... Yes. I was very lonely. I needed to get away...

As soon as I got the chance, I moved to the United States.

For registration, go over there...

US CUSTOMS and IMMIGRATION

I met Harry... also a survivor.

So are you from Germany or Holland?

It's moeilijk... uh, complicated.

Bagels 15 ct

We got married and had two children, Paul and Rose.

Come'n Get It

But I never stopped missing my parents.

Blow out the candles and make a wish! Happy Birthday, dear Paulie...

Pfffffffffff...

HAPPY BIRTHDAY PAULIE

I could never talk about the war... even with Harry.

28

Now I want to tell my whole family about what happened back then...

I'm glad you came to visit me...

We should be going now... It's been quite an exhausting day.

That evening...

See you next time!

At Daniel's house...

...afterwards, Gran never saw Bob again...

What a sad story...

Hey, wait a second...

...Canter with a C, I think...

A Canter family Web site...!

ANYBODY KNOW A BOB CANTER FROM AMSTERDAM WHO SURVIVED AUSCHWITZ?

Bleep!

You have mail !

Gran, Gran! I found Bob Canter! On a Web site. He lives in Israel. His granddaughter just gave me his telephone number!

Huh, what did you say? What time is it?

That morning...

Hello... Bob Canter?

Yes...?

It's Esther, Esther Hecht, from Holland...

Excuse me, Esther...?

A while later...

I just spoke to Bob. It's unbelievable! He remembers so much about my parents. I'm going to see him.

Let me go with you?

A few days later...

Are you okay, Mom?

I'm not looking forward to this, but I need to know.

A week later...

Helena, I'm back from Israel. I have so much to tell you. When can I come over?

Later on...

It was very special to see him again...

Bob and his granddaughter came and picked us up at the airport.

Esther...

Bob...

Bob, how amazing to see each other again. After all these years...

Thanks to our grandchildren and the Internet.

A while later...

I live here...

That afternoon...

Look, here they are. I already have great-grandchildren.

PHOTOS
FAMILY ALBUM
PICTURE BOOK
FOTO ALBUM

It was evening before we found the courage to delve into the past...

Okay... Where to begin...

We talked through the night.

Bob knew even more about my parents than I imagined.

It all started with that awful roundup.

When are we going to eat lunch? I have to meet some friends.

Keep that music down, Bob.

MARK TW

ACHTUNG! ATTENTION!

WOOF WOOF

VROAAAM VROOM

What is that?!

A razzia!

Oh no!

...PREPARE FOR TRANSPORT...

My parents were also taken away.

Esther! She's still at school!

Schneller! Faster!

Then they saw Helena's father. He had been dispatched to help the Germans.

Look!

Our neighbor!

Nazi!

Keep moving!

Esther's at school. Help us?!

I'll see what I can do.

The neighbors stood by...

We can't help them.

Where are they being taken?

To the Dutch Theatre.

My parents were taken to the Dutch Theatre. That was a sort of depot for Jews who had been rounded up.

Everybody was registered there.

We once saw splendid plays in this theatre, and now...

Bob heard my parents talking about me...

Karl and Miriam Hecht.

We're worried about Esther...

Did they ever know that you went into hiding?

No, probably not.

The theatre was jam-packed!

Hey, my mother needs to sit down!

I'm so tired. Please get me something to drink, Bob.

Why isn't Esther here yet?

Maybe Helena's father can't find her...

LOGE

BALKON

Maurits! You're here too?

I help distribute food and post the mail to avoid being deported, at least for the time being.

I'm here with my parents. Any idea when we're being transported?

You're leaving for Westerbork in a day or so.

And after that to eastern Europe to work...

They say that everyone is killed there...

I know a way to get out of here.

Maurits explained that Jewish Council* members removed names from the list.

*Jewish organization that was forced to assist in the deportation of Jews.

If you could get off the list, it was possible to escape.

Over the fence! Someone will take you to a safe address for the night.

Shhhh!

I can help you. We'll hide you until the transport has left. Do you know a place where you can go into hiding?

LOGE

What now? How to find a safe address?

My legs won't hold me anymore...

No, I can't leave them alone. They need me.

The next morning...

We have to do this, while we still can...

Sob... Judith...

We're in touch with the Resistance.

She's only 5 months old...

A hard labor camp is no place for a baby...

34

When you're put on the transport, we'll give you a doll... so the count is correct.

I don't know if I can do this.

What were they talking about?

Whether their baby should be hidden.

Children younger than thirteen went to a day nursery, opposite the Dutch Theatre.

Only one German SS soldier was stationed on the other side of the street. So at times the Resistance could smuggle children out of the nursery.

You ready?

Yes...

The perfect moment was when the streetcar pulled up to the stop...

Now!

Around 600 children were saved... but the rest were transported to the camps.

C'mon, darlings. Hurry!

That evening, the orders to leave arrived.

I wonder if her baby is with her.

The train to Westerbork...

You're back on the job?

So?

Some of our co-workers won't do these runs.

Doesn't matter to me one way or the other! I need the money!

Me too! Besides, if we don't do it, somebody else will!

At Camp Westerbork...

Let's try to stay together.

Yes...

A while later...

Here's where we sleep?

We're right down there.

Do we have to stay here long?

I really don't know...

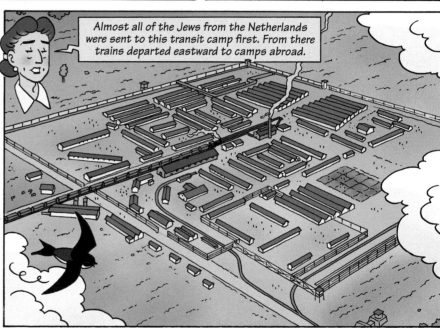

Almost all of the Jews from the Netherlands were sent to this transit camp first. From there trains departed eastward to camps abroad.

Bob quickly understood how things were done in Westerbork.

You work here until it's your turn to go.

Bob's father had to break apart shot-down planes.

Our mothers had to make clothing.

My father worked as a doctor. He managed to get Bob a job in the camp hospital.

That's where Bob met Chaja.

Could you help me?

Of course.

It was love at first sight.

Under control?

Sure...

Mumblemm... stop! My head... mmmbl...

Mmblmmbl...

I'm frightened. They say we'll be killed in eastern Europe... Could it be true?

Ah, you hear so much.

Prior to departure, the names of people who would be transported were read aloud.

...Jetta Hansen, Anton Hoogstede, Roosje Hoogstede, Bram Hoogstede...

Luckily, not us...

Then one evening...

BOB! I have to leave... on tomorrow's transport!

When this is all over, we'll see each other again in Amsterdam...

Sob... Yes, okay ...sob!

Those who stayed behind were confined to the barracks.

Chaja! Bye, my love!

A few weeks later...

...Karl Hecht, Miriam Hecht, Sara Hildekamp...

You too...!

Are those sick people and elderly also going?

They're in no shape to work!

That pail is the toilet?

Come quickly, so we can get a place by the hatch for some fresh air!

The number of people inside was written on each boxcar.

K-AUSCHWITZ-WESTERBORK
GESCHLOSSEN

The train carrying my parents left for eastern Europe with more than 1,000 people: Jewish men, women, and children.

Farewell letters were thrown from the train. People who lived in the area often mailed them.

Dear Aunt and Uncle, We're on the train. We're very brave. So please don't worry. We have no idea where we're headed. Betty and Jacob.

How long is the trip?

I can't breathe!

No idea...

Don't push!

Careful! It's hard for her to stand.

Sit on these suitcases.

A day later...

The pail is full. The stench...

It can't be much longer.

After a while...

Empty the pails! Fetch water!

This isn't nearly over...

They were robbed on the way.

Your money and jewelry!

SCHNELL!

Three days later, everyone was totally exhausted.

So now what's next?

They were on their way to Auschwitz, a Nazi death camp in occupied Poland.

The reality of what had gone on in eastern Europe only became clear after the war.

Hitler had decided at the end of 1941 that all 11 million Jews in Europe were to be murdered.

Yes, my Führer.

In January 1942, senior Nazi officials met in Berlin. There they discussed how to systematically murder all of Europe's Jews.

Reinhard Heydrich chaired the meeting.

We have accomplished a lot in the past two years in eastern Europe. But it is not enough...

In occupied Poland, more than 100,000 Jews lived locked away in so-called ghettos.

WOHNGEBIET DER JUDEN BETRETEN VERBOTEN

By 1941, Germany had invaded the Soviet Union. About 3 million Jews lived there.

Hitler had special army units in the Soviet Union. These "Einsatzgruppen" had orders to shoot and kill as many Jews as possible.

You are doing this for our Führer and Fatherland.

In just over a year, 1.5 million Jewish men, women, and children were shot dead there.

Yesterday 3,000 Jews, today twice as many. We can be proud!

Dirty job. But we've got our orders.

All these women and children... I can't stomach it. I need to get out of here!

Shooting takes too long. There are far better methods to kill the Jews.

SS OberGp.[

The Nazis decided to build more death camps in occupied Poland. Large numbers of people could be killed there in a very short time.

Treblinka

Kulmhof

Sobibor
Majdanek
Belzec
Auschwitz

Of course, the plan had to be kept secret...

We'll just keep saying that the Jews are being sent to labor camps.

They must continue believing this...

Then they won't fight back.

Adolf Eichmann was put in charge of organizing the deportation of all of Europe's Jews to the death camps.

Within a few months, trains from all over Europe were on their way to these camps. Auschwitz was the largest one.

Westerbork

Auschwitz

A total of 107,000 Jews from the Netherlands were deported to the camps. Only 5,000 survived.

Most people thought they were going to labor camps. But some people didn't believe it...

How can Mom work? She's totally exhausted.

We've stopped...

I see a sign... Auschwitz... Is this it?

41

Bob could still clearly remember arriving at Auschwitz...

WOOF WOOF WOOF!

We need to stay together...

Leave your luggage!

GET OUT !!! SCHNELLER!

Is she dead?

Keep moving.

Sixteen... Say you're sixteen!

Why did he say that?

Anyone younger was gassed immediately.

Women and children right, men to the left.

Don't worry. You'll soon be reunited...

But that wasn't true? They were actually...

Yes, but people couldn't know it. This way they didn't panic.

An SS doctor determined which men and women were fit enough to work. Bob, his father, and my father passed the selection. Our mothers didn't...

Right...

Rudolf Höss was the Commandant of Auschwitz.

A large group this time. Where are they from?

From the Netherlands, sir...

Your youngest son was at my daughter's birthday party, right?

Yes, he enjoyed himself.

Höss lived with his wife and five children right next to the camp.

Kids grow up fast.

Let's have a drink, shall we?

In the meantime...

Schneller! Faster!

A number was tattooed on everyone's arm.

Ouch...

unters

Then the prisoners' heads were completely shaved.

They got camp clothing.

One shoe is too big, and the other's too small!

Father... is it you?

Oh, Bob... my boy!

Why did they do that?

To make you feel less than human. From then on, you were just a number.

Bob and the others were herded off to the barracks.

About 700 people slept in one barrack. Sometimes four men had to sleep in one bunk.

What a stench...

So, we sleep here?

Hurry, or we won't have anywhere to sleep.

Where are our wives?

Gone...

When Bob told me that, I realized what had happened to my mother.

After the selection...

Don't be afraid...

You're all filthy from the trip. First go take a shower.

You can undress downstairs. Remember the number of the hook where you hang up your clothing.

Tie your shoes together, so you won't lose them...

See you later...

They thought it was a shower...

But poison gas pellets were dropped through the ceiling. In 15 minutes everyone was dead.

Their clothing was gathered and searched for valuables.

My mother was gassed and her body burned in a crematorium...

Day and night, Bob saw the smoking chimneys.

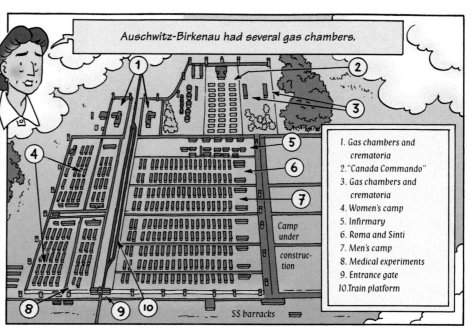

Auschwitz-Birkenau had several gas chambers.

Camp under construction

1. Gas chambers and crematoria
2. "Canada Commando"
3. Gas chambers and crematoria
4. Women's camp
5. Infirmary
6. Roma and Sinti
7. Men's camp
8. Medical experiments
9. Entrance gate
10. Train platform

SS barracks

Bob ended up in the men's camp with other Jews and also political prisoners, mainly from Poland and Russia.

To są Holendrzy...*

*They're from Holland.

Auschwitz-Birkenau was also a labor camp. The Nazis wanted the prisoners to work themselves to death.

What were they forced to do?

Well, a bit of everything... building roads, working in a munitions factory, building barracks...

The day began before dawn at 4 a.m.

Wake up! Roll call! Schnell, schneller!!!

First the prisoners were counted. They often stood for hours.

Then the real work would begin. Bob and our fathers had to lug heavy stones.

Son, I won't make it!

If you quit, they'll shoot you!

Once when Bob tried to help somebody, he was badly beaten.

Back to work!!

Those guards were awful!

They were prisoners themselves, forced to work as guards.

There was constant hunger.

It's not much.

They got soup for lunch. But it was little more than water with potato peels.

Most people died within three months.

This is a nightmare...

But Bob survived...

Bob was lucky. Certain jobs in the camp were less strenuous. Bob ended up in the so-called "Canada Commando."

The first time Bob went to work there, he could barely believe his eyes...

What a pile of clothing!

Knowing Chaja was alive gave Bob strength to keep going.

Sigh...

Z Z Z

CHAJA

One morning a prisoner was missing his cap.

Where is it?!!

Bob saw the man steal another cap...

A bit later...

What? No cap?!

BANG

You got shot for something like that?

Bob's father was not doing very well...

Bob, I can't go on anymore!

C'mon, Dad. Don't give up!

I must get some extra bread tomorrow...

One day after work...

What's keeping Dad? The rest of his group has already returned.

Where's my father?

His wheelbarrow with stones tipped over... They beat him to death...

...!

Now I'm alone...

Don't give up, Bob. There's still Chaja... and we have each other.

My father and Bob helped each other.

Hang on... It won't last much longer...

A few weeks later, my father got lucky.

Bob! I'm going to work in the infirmary!

That work was less physical.

Doctor, help me!

I'm trying, but we don't have any medicine.

People who were too sick and too weak were simply sent to the gas chambers.

Him too...

Poor soul, I can't do anything for him...

Which number is he?

In the spring of 1944...

Unbelievable! All these bags! Where did they all come from?

Someone just told me...

The luggage was from 440,000 Hungarian Jews who had been deported to Auschwitz.

Most of them were gassed immediately.

But wasn't there ever an uprising?

Of course...

A few hundred prisoners set a crematorium on fire.
But it wasn't a fair fight.

All those who took part were shot.

The revolt was extraordinary, given that most prisoners were sick and too weak to even fight back.

Also, the guards were always watching and the fences were electrified.

But sometimes someone did escape.

What are they doing with them?

Someone escaped from their barrack. Now they're all going to be killed.

Escaped prisoners told the British and American governments about Auschwitz. But little was done by the Allies with that information.

Bob saw more and more Allied bombers flying overhead.

Why don't they bomb the gas chambers and the railway lines?

Stay in formation. Approaching target!

Bombardier calling. I see a vast camp complex.

Our assignment is to bomb the factories to the east of here.

Unbelievable!!!

They should have bombed the gas chambers!

Bob was worried about Chaja. She no longer answered his notes...

Don't start thinking the worst. Maybe she's been transferred.

By the end of 1944, it was apparent that Germany was losing the war.

It can't last much longer.

Let's hope not!

Listen... The Russians are getting closer!

The Nazis started blowing up the gas chambers and crematoria. They burned as many documents as possible.

They're destroying the evidence of their crimes.

So they were then freed by the Russians?

No. Their suffering still wasn't over.

The prisoners, including my father and Bob, were forced to leave the camp.

It was the dead of winter and freezing cold. Nobody had warm clothing or good shoes.

Where are they taking us?

No idea.

It was hard for my father...

Try to hang on! Otherwise they'll shoot you!

Please, Bob, help me...

Get up! Or you die too!

I... Wait, he...

BANG

That's how my father died...

And Bob? What happened to him?

They stumbled on for days. Many died.

Here! Some bread!

Stay out of this!

Then they were loaded onto a train.

Schneller!

After a harsh journey they reached Germany.

Hey! What's that?

The Americans thought they were German soldiers...

A huge panic broke out. Bob and a few others grabbed their chance.

C'mon... let's go...!

They escaped.

They roamed through the forest. They were exhausted. Suddenly...

...they walked right into the arms of American soldiers!

Don't shoot! Don't shoot!

They got some food and drink.

They searched the abandoned houses of Germans for clothing and more food.

I'm feeling a bit better...

Bob couldn't stop thinking about his parents and Chaja...

Then early in May 1945, the news arrived: Germany had surrendered!

Peace!!!

At last!

Hurrah!!!

Not much to celebrate...

I know, I'm all alone as well...

And what finally happened to Hitler? And to the guards?

Hitler committed suicide. Most of the guards were never punished.

And so what did Bob do next?

Bob wanted to return to Amsterdam.

Chaja...

Everybody aboard? Then we can get going.

Will I ever see Chaja again?

55

During this trip, Bob saw much of Germany in ruins.

How will it be in the Netherlands?

What camp were you in?

Bergen-Belsen...

I lost my husband and children...

My parents are dead. I'm hoping my girlfriend...

You're at the Dutch border. How long have you been away?

About 2 years... but it feels like a lifetime.

THIS IS HOLLAND THE DUTCH ARE OUR ALLIES

Bob finally arrived.

Amsterdam...

But because he no longer had a family or a home, he slept at a relief center.

What a homecoming...

Nobody really wants to hear about what happened to us.

He asked everywhere about Chaja. Then one day...

Chaja was a friend of mine. She's not coming back...

Bob saw my ad in the paper...

Esther! She's alive...

I've got to tell her the horrible truth...

After an hour he went on his way... disappeared out of my life.

Bob later emigrated to Israel, where he could build a new life.

MS NEGBAH
נגבה

He helped establish a new village and he still lives there today.

Phew... this heat.

Bob met his wife, Rifka, there.

A few years ago, Bob went to Auschwitz with his entire family.

What? Does it still exist?

Yes, the gate and many barracks are still there...

It's a monument to all the people who perished there.

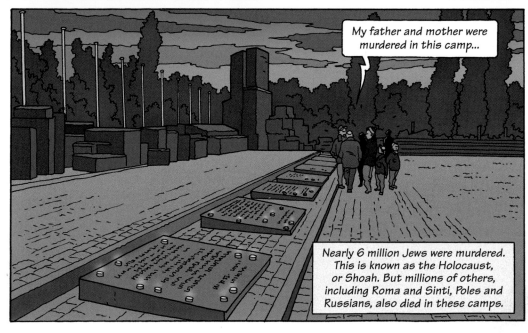

My father and mother were murdered in this camp...

Nearly 6 million Jews were murdered. This is known as the Holocaust, or Shoah. But millions of others, including Roma and Sinti, Poles and Russians, also died in these camps.

And like Bob, I've spent my entire life missing my parents terribly...

57

I have nothing to remind me of them... I can barely remember their faces...

...

I can't believe I didn't think of this sooner!

Wait... Wait just a...

BOOM!!!

You okay, Gran?!

Mumble... mumble. It must be here somewhere...

What is it, Gran?

...or am I mistaken?

58

After the roundup, I went to their apartment...

I knew the Germans would have the place emptied.

I'd better be quick...

I went searching for something personal, a keepsake...

Yes... this!

It has to be here somewhere...

OUCH!!! ...Gran!

Oops, sorry!

YESSSS!

?!?

I have... still... saved...

Aaaah...

Text copyright © 2007 by Anne Frank Stichting, Amsterdam
Artwork copyright © 2007 by Eric Heuvel, Redhill Illustrations
English translation copyright © 2007 by Lorraine T. Miller
The Search was originally published in Dutch by the Anne Frank House in cooperation
with the Jewish Historical Museum of Amsterdam under the title *De Zoektocht*
Published in agreement with the Anne Frank House
Printed in May 2009 in China by South China Printing Co. Ltd.,
Dongguan City, Guangdong Province
Published simultaneously in hardcover and paperback
First American edition, 2009
1   3   5   7   9   10   8   6   4   2

www.fsgkidsbooks.com

Library of Congress Cataloging-in-Publication Data
Heuvel, Eric, 1960–
    [Zoektocht. English]
    The search / Eric Heuvel ; Ruud van der Rol ; Lies Schippers ; [English translation by Lorraine T.
Miller].— 1st American ed.
        p.   cm.
    Summary: After recounting her experience as a Jewish girl living in Amsterdam during the
Holocaust, Esther, helped by her grandson, embarks on a search to discover what happened to
her parents before they died in a concentration camp.
    ISBN: 978-0-374-36517-2 (hardcover)
    1. Holocaust, Jewish (1939–1945)—Juvenile fiction. [1. Holocaust, Jewish (1939–1945)—Fiction.
2. Holocaust survivors—Fiction. 3. Jews—Netherlands—Fiction. 4. Grandmothers—Fiction.]
I. Rol, Ruud van der. II. Schippers, Lies. III. Miller, Lorraine T. IV. Title.

PZ7.H444Se 2009
[Fic]—dc22
                                                                                            2009013603

Scenario
Eric Heuvel
Ruud van der Rol
Lies Schippers
Drawings
Eric Heuvel / Redhill Illustrations
Translated from the Dutch by
Lorraine T. Miller / Epicycles
Coloring
J & M Colorstudio
Creative Support and Documentation
Jacqueline Koerts / Redhill Illustrations
Design
Karel Oosting
Production
Anne Frank House

A special thanks goes to Annemiek Gringold
(Hollandsche Schouwburg / Dutch Theatre Memorial Centre)
for contributing her expertise in the development
of the scenario.

The Search was originally published in Dutch as
De Zoektocht, thanks in part to funding provided by the
Ministry of Public Health, Welfare and Sport (VWS)
in the Netherlands.

Many others also offered their comments and advice
in the development of the scenario:

Content Experts (The Netherlands)
R. C. Musaph-Andriesse (Advisory Council, Anne Frank House);
Liesbeth van der Horst (Resistance Museum Amsterdam);
Dirk Mulder, Erik Guns (Memorial Center Camp Westerbork);
Nine Nooter (National Committee May 4th and 5th);
René Kok, Erik Somers (Netherlands Institute for War
Documentation / NIOD);
Jeroen van der Eijnde (National Monument Camp Vught);
Femke Akerboom (Markt 12 Museum, Aalten);
Ido Abram (Learning Foundation, Amsterdam);
Joost van Bodegom (Chairman Resistance Museum);
Joël Cahen, Petra Katzenstein, Léontine Meijer
(Jewish Historical Museum / Amsterdam);
Menno Metselaar, Marian Stegeman, Mieke Sobering
(Anne Frank House).

Content Experts (International)
Paul Salmons (Imperial War Museum, Great Britain);
Wolf Kaiser (Wannsee Conference House Memorial, Germany);
Claude Singer and Philippe Boukara (Shoah Memorial, France);
Mirosław Obstarczyk (Auschwitz State Museum, Poland);
Piotr Trojanski (German-Polish Center, Poland);
Monica Kovács (Hannah Arendt Association, Hungary);
Werner Dreier (National Socialism and the Holocaust: Memory
and Present, Austria).